D0459761

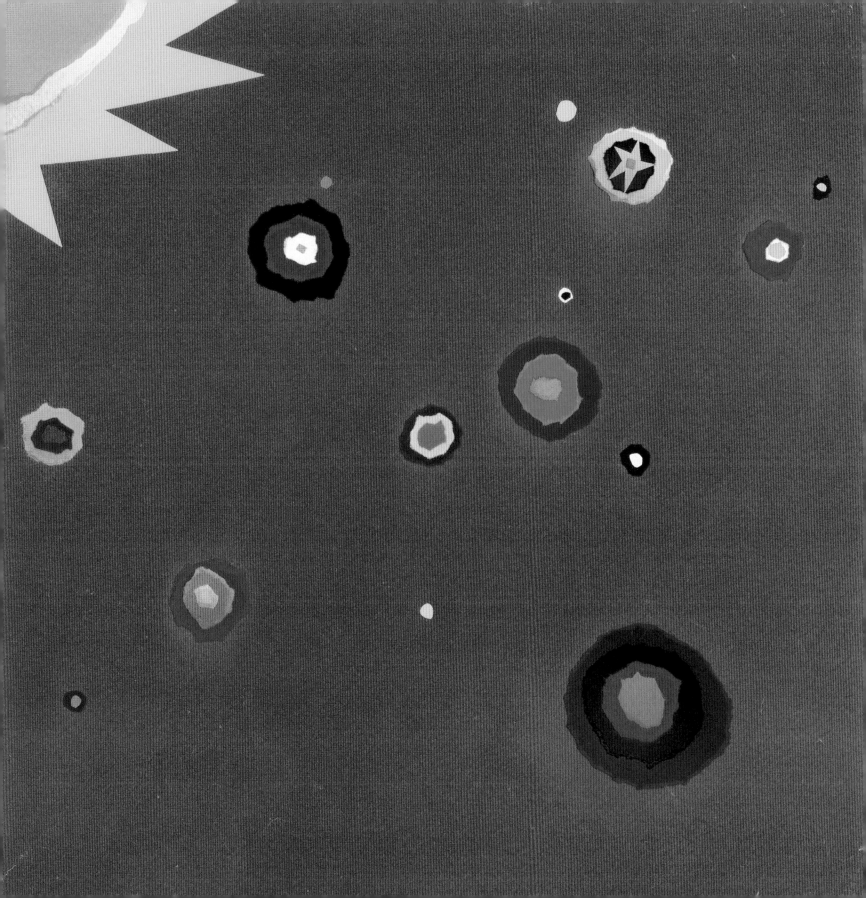

To Everything

To everything
Jean, Joe, & Catherine
have done for me.
— B.B.

©1998 by Bob Barner.
All rights reserved.
"A Guide To Using This Book," ©1998 by Chronicle Books,
is based on the "Chronicle Books Study Guide" by Belle Akers.

Book design by Cathleen O'Brien.
Original text type designed by Kathy Warinner.
The illustrations in this book were rendered in paper collage.
Printed in Hong Kong.

Library of Congress Cataloging-in-Publication Data

Bob Barner
    To Everything / by Bob Barner
        p.   cm.
    Summary: Presents an illustrated version of the verse in Ecclesiastes which states
that there is a time for everything, including a time to be born and a time to die.
    ISBN 0-8118-2086-6
    1. Bible. O.T. Ecclesiastes III, 2-8—Paraphrases, English—Juvenile literature.
[1. Bible. O.T. Ecclesiastes. 2. Seasons.]   1. Title.
BS1476.B28 1998
223'809505—dc21   98-11107
                        CIP
                        AC

Distributed in Canada by Raincoast Books
8680 Cambie Street, Vancouver, British Columbia V6P 6M9

10 9 8 7 6 5 4 3 2 1

Chronicle Books
85 Second Street, San Francisco, California 94105

www.chroniclebooks.com

3 3056 00552 7166

To Everything

Bob Barner

chronicle books · san francisco

To everything
and a time
under

there is a season,
to every purpose
the heavens.

A time to be born,

a time
to die.

A time to plant,

a time to pick.

A time to tear apart

a time to sew together.

A time to cry,

a time to laugh.

A time to mourn,

a time to dance.

A time to give,

A time to hold

a time to let go.

A time to be silent,

a time to speak.

a time for anger.

A time for war,

a time for
peace.

chere is a season,
o every purpose
he heavens.

A note from the author

To Everything is based on the book of Ecclesiastes from the Old Testament. This verse has always been a favorite of mine and is one of the first I remember hearing as a child. As a young adult, I sang along with the words in the form of popular songs.

Many versions of the verse exist. I have chosen to illustrate those passages that I felt were most universal. The pages of this book are designed to convey the message that these events and the feelings they evoke are natural and that there truly is a season, a time, and a purpose for everything.

I hope that the images I have created will bring you much joy and will help make the timeless message of these wise words accessible to readers of all ages and backgrounds.

Bob Barner

A guide to using this book

To Everything captures love, hope, and joy as well as the conflict that inevitably occurs in the course of life. Bob Barner's colorful paper collages beautifully illustrate a simple verse that has powerful meaning. The brightly colored illustrations convey emotions that are all a part of the human spirit.

To Everything can be used as a springboard for discussions about the choices we make and the effects of our actions upon others. These discussions may take place upon a single reading of the book or over a period of time as different parts of the verse are explored.

As the book is read aloud, allow extra time for children to look closely at the illustrations. After a complete reading of the book, go back to the beginning and have discussions related to each page. Children will enjoy talking about all the things they see in the illustrations.

Focus Questions
• Look at the colors and shapes on each page. What captures your attention? Do the images help you understand the meaning of the words more clearly? How?

Activity
The art in this book was done in paper collage. The papers were torn by hand or cut with scissors and glued down. Make your own collage with colored papers, magazine pages, newspaper, or things like buttons or used stamps. Give your collage a name and describe what it's about.

Cycles

To Everything shows that changes are a part of life. Several passages relate to cycles – "To everything there is a season"; "A time to be born, a time to die"; and "A time to plant, a time to pick" – are wonderful springboards to science discussions.

Focus Questions
• The seasons follow a cycle and change in the same order once a year. Can you name the seasons? What are some things that happen in each season? Do you feel differently during different seasons?
• What are some other things in life that follow a cycle?

Activity
Create a collage to show your favorite season.

Feelings

Feelings and emotions are natural. Some emotions are strong and can be expressed by crying or yelling; others are quiet and may not be expressed as easily. Discuss ways that people show different emotions. Share personal experiences related to strong emotions, such as sadness, joy, love, and anger.

Focus Questions
• Think about a time when you have cried. What made you cry? What made you feel better? Think about a time when you laughed. What made you laugh?
• Are there times when you have felt angry? What caused that feeling? What made you less angry?
• What are ways to show love? How do you show love to others?

Activity
Create a collage that expresses a feeling, like being happy or sad.

Giving and Receiving

Many of the verses in the book relate to the idea of giving and receiving. Mother birds give nourishment to their chicks; lions protect their cubs. Every day, by interacting with others, we give and we receive.

Focus Questions
• What does it mean to give and to receive? When are times that people may give something to others or receive something from others?
• Share a time when you have given something or received something. How did it make you feel?
• Giving and receiving are not always about presents. What other things do people give and receive?

Activity
Use collage materials to create a card for someone.

Resolving Conflicts

People have opinions that express their point of view. When people can't agree or don't share each other's point of view, conflicts arise. Sometimes people are able to work together and reach an agreement. When this doesn't happen, conflicts can result in physical actions such as yelling, fighting, or even in war.

Focus Questions
• Share a personal conflict you have had. How did you respond? How was the conflict resolved?
• What are some ways people can work together to resolve conflicts?

Activity
Create a collage that shows people working together.

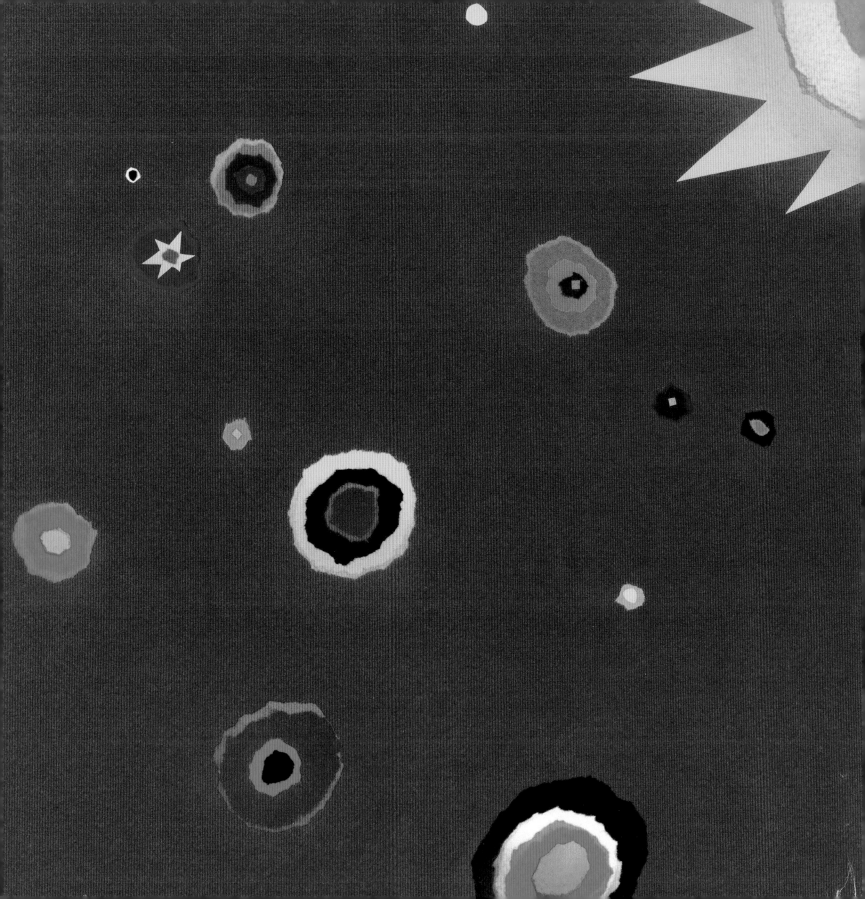